PUMPKIN CARVING FOR SUPERSTITIOUS WITCHES

AN OBSCURE ACADEMY STORY

LAURA GREENWOOD

Happy Reading!
Laura Greenwood

© 2022 Laura Greenwood

All rights reserved. This book or parts thereof may not be reproduced in any form, stored in any retrieval system, or transmitted in any form by any means – electronic, mechanical, photocopy, recording or otherwise – without prior written permission of the published, except as provided by United States of America copyright law. For permission requests, write to the publisher at "Attention: Permissions Coordinator," at the email address; lauragreenwood@authorlauragreenwood.co.uk.

Visit Laura Greenwood's website at:

www.authorlauragreenwood.co.uk

Cover by Ravenborn Designs

Pumpkin Carving For Superstitious Witches is a work of fiction. Names, characters, places, and incidents are the products of the author's imagination or are used fictitiously. Any resemblance to actual persons, living or dead, businesses, companies, events, or locales is entirely coincidental.

If you find an error, you can report it via my website. Please note that my books are written in British English: https://www.authorlauragreenwood.co.uk/p/report-error.html

To keep up to date with new releases, sales, and other updates, you can join my mailing list via my website or The Paranormal Council Reader Group on Facebook.

BLURB

If there's one thing Juniper always does for Halloween, it's making sure her door is guarded by a Jack-'o-lantern.

But when her pumpkin is removed by building services, she's left with a few hours to find a new one and carve it.

But finding a pumpkin on Halloween is harder than it sounds, and she's about to give up when Emmett appears and helps her find an alternative.

Can the two of them get the Jack-o'-lantern carved in time?

-

Pumpkin Carving For Suspicious Witches is a light-hearted witch academy m/f romance set at Obscure Academy. It is Juniper and Emmett's complete story.

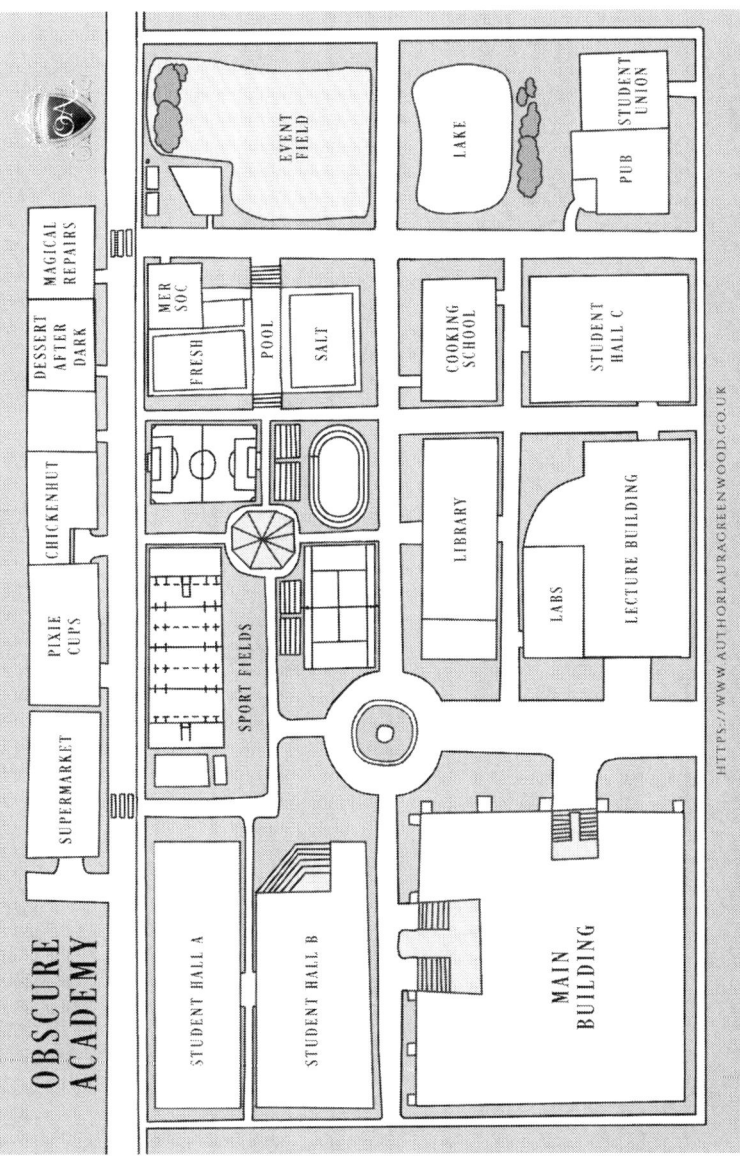

ONE

Juniper

I scrape the inside of my pumpkin, being careful to remove as much of the flesh as possible. While it's only a byproduct of my main goal with carving the Jack o' lantern, I do like pumpkin cake, and I plan on making a delicious one out of this.

It'll be a nice accompaniment to staying inside with a good book and a cup of tea tomorrow night.

"Hey, Juniper," Thalia says as she enters the kitchen, heading straight to the fridge.

"Hey," I respond.

"It's looking good." She nods to the pumpkin as she grabs a smoothie.

I chuckle. "There's no need to be polite, it looks like a pumpkin and a pile of guts."

She shuts the fridge door. "That's fair. But it looks better than an hour ago."

"Just wait and see how it looks tomorrow," I say with pride.

"Is there a reason you're not using magic to scoop it all out?" she asks.

I shrug. "Sometimes it's better to do things by hand." Especially when it's a Jack-o'-lantern meant to help protect me from the spirits of the dead.

She nods, seeming to accept my answer at face value. "Are you sure we can't convince you to come out with us?"

I shake my head. "I'm surprised you're going."

"Michaela and Evander convinced me."

"Ah." It's a shame, the two of us had a good time hiding out and not going partying on Halloween last year. She's become a lot more outgoing since she went to the blind dating event a few months ago.

"You could still change your mind and come if you want," Thalia says. "All of Michaela's flatmates are going, they're normally a lot of fun. And everyone's dressing up."

"I'm okay, thanks." I smile reassuringly at her, hoping she drops it.

Confusion passes over her face, and I don't blame

her. "Can I ask why you don't like Halloween?"

"You can." I didn't expect her to ask, but mostly because no one ever has before and not because I don't want to talk about it.

"Will you tell me the answer?" She sits down opposite me while I keep working on my pumpkin.

"I don't dislike Halloween," I admit. "It's more that Halloween doesn't like me."

"You've lost me."

I let out a loud sigh, struggling to find the words to explain myself that doesn't make me sound like I'm making things up. Which is the main reason I've never really talked about this before. "My family has always been sensitive to the dead."

"I thought you were a witch."

"I am. I can't talk to the dead, but they make it hard to do anything on days when the veil between the dead and the living is thinner."

"Like Halloween."

And a few other days in the year, some of which might surprise people who aren't sensitive to this kind of thing.

"Exactly. So I carve myself a Jack o'lantern to keep the bad spirits away, and keep to myself so nothing bothers me. It means missing out on Halloween fun, but better that than being bombarded by the constant whispers of spirits and never quite being able to work out what they're saying." Which can unsurprisingly get very frustrating at times.

"That doesn't seem particularly fun," Thalia responds.

"It's not," I agreed. "Granny taught me the right way to carve a pumpkin when I was seven. It makes me feel close to her." A pang of loss flew through me at the thought of her. I wished she was still with us.

"Is there any particular face that's best?" she asks. "Or should it be symbols instead?"

"I normally do a traditional face." I set down the carving spoon I'm using to scoop out the insides and grab the marker I brought earlier. Carefully, I outline the face I'm planning on doing, with jagged teeth and triangles for eyes.

"Ah, a classic." Thalia nods.

"I've done more unique ones before, but I always end up worrying that it isn't going to work as well and then carve the traditional style face as before, so it's better just go straight for this one."

"That makes sense. You have to do what's best for you."

I nod. "I know it might seem silly..."

"Trust me, it doesn't. I did a lot of things because I didn't want my condition to get in the way." She adjusts her glasses.

"Your condition?"

"I'm a gorgon."

Understanding dawns on me. "Ah, yes, I can see how that would cause some complications."

"Which is why it makes sense to me that you're taking this seriously. I'd do the same in your position."

I smile at her, enjoying that she doesn't think I'm weird, and feeling reassured that I live with someone who understands what it means to have something that worries me. Not that I think any of my flatmates would be cruel about my choices. I wouldn't have elected to live with them again for second year if I'd thought that was the case, and while some of them have moved on to other flats, most of them have stayed here. It's nice to have friendly faces around.

Thalia's phone goes off and she pulls it out, checking the message. "Evander's outside waiting to let me in," she says. "But I look forward to seeing your pumpkin when it's finished."

"Thanks. I'll send you a photo if you want?"

She nods. "Please, I'd love to see it."

"I'll make sure to," I promise, enjoying the idea that someone else is interested in seeing what I'm creating, even if it's not that exciting.

She waves goodbye and heads back out of the kitchen, presumably to go and let her boyfriend in.

I turn my attention back to the pumpkin, losing myself in the rhythm of scraping out the insides. I'm not sure how long it takes me, but I'm relieved by the point where I realise I can start working on carving the face.

I swap my scoop for a small knife and carefully make the initial cuts along the outline I did earlier. I hum to myself as I work, enjoying the way it's coming together. Even if the process made me feel close to my Grandma, I still found it tedious the first few times she made me do it with her. Probably because I was only small at the time and didn't have the same patience or understanding for the whole thing as I do now.

I set down my knife and use my thumb to push the loose triangle of pumpkin through. At first, it resists, but after a moment, it falls through. I repeat the process on the other one before moving to the nose and mouth.

Within ten minutes, I have a tea light flickering inside my pumpkin, lighting up the face and causing a dancing glow to spread across the table.

I pull out my phone and take a photo. I send it to Thalia before adding it to my family chat.

< I'm all set for tomorrow! >

A photo pops up in response from my brother with a pumpkin of his own. < Me too! >

I smile to myself, reassured that I'm not the only one who has spent the night before Halloween focusing on my pumpkin and not something that others would deem more important.

I leave the light flickering and turn my attention to the scooped-out pumpkin flesh, feeling better now I'm done and prepared for tomorrow. I pull up the Broomstick Bakery blog and search for the pumpkin cake recipe they shared a few years ago. I hope it's included in the recipe book they've just published, but I won't find out until I get it for Christmas from my parents.

I grab flour from the cupboard and start making the batter for my pumpkin cake. If last year was anything to go by, I'm going to have to double the recipe and make a lot of cake to ensure all of my flatmates get enough. But I like it. Doing this for them makes me feel like I'm part of the group. I know no one would ever say that I wasn't anyway, nor do they make me feel like I'm not, but I think it's hard to remember sometimes when I'm passing on nights out like Halloween.

I push the thought aside. It's one night, and one of them now knows why I'm like this. I have nothing to worry about. Except for the dead, that is.

TWO

Emmett

"Hey, will you hold the door?" someone calls.

I step to the side and hold open the door to the lecture room, turning to find a frazzled-looking Juniper hurrying towards me.

She lets out a loud sigh when she recognises me. "Hey, Emmett."

"Morning," I respond. "I'm guessing you have M2S. too?" Not that it'll be worth getting out of bed for. The *Marketing to Supernaturals* module sounds interesting on paper, but is so bogged down in the theory that it's incredibly dull. The best part of the lecture is that I often get to spend time with Juniper, who seems to hold the lecturer in the same amount of esteem as I do, which isn't saying much.

"Mmhmm. I thought I set my alarm, but somehow, I still only woke up twenty minutes ago. I dread to think what I look like." She pushes a strand of dark brown hair behind her ear.

"I wouldn't have known if you hadn't told me," I assure her, meaning every word of it. She always looks cute, even when she's wearing nothing fancier than jeans and a t-shirt.

"I'm flattered, but I'm pretty sure that isn't true." She flashes me a shy smile that I think might mean she's truly appreciative of the compliment.

We make our way through the corridor and towards the entrance to the lecture hall. She pushes on the door and holds it open for me, gesturing for me to head through.

"Thanks," I say.

"Just returning the favour."

"Still preferable to having the door slam in my face."

She lets out a small snort of amusement. "Has that happened to you?"

"Once, but it was my sister after I hexed her hair."

"You didn't?" She's almost full-out laughing now, making her more adorable than ever. I'm not sure what it is about her, but she always makes me feel warm and fuzzy inside.

I wish I had the courage to ask her on a date, but I haven't figured out the way yet.

"I did. I apologised afterwards, but I thought it would be funny to hex her hair so that every time she used her brush, it would change the colour."

"How old were you?"

I frown. "I'm not sure, maybe eight or nine."

"That's pretty advanced magic, I know a lot of people who'd pay good money to a witchy hairdresser for that," she says, seeming genuinely impressed.

"I hadn't thought about it like that. I just wanted to wind her up." I gesture to one of the rows of benches and she slips in, making no move to go and sit with anyone else. I know she has other friends in the class, but I like it when she sits with me.

"I hope she gave as good as she got."

I let out a low chuckle. "Believe me, she did. Just before I started secondary school, she cursed me so that every time I said my name, I croaked like a frog."

A small smile lifts the corners of Juniper's lips. "That's funny."

"I'm glad you think so."

"Can you still do it?"

"Only as a party trick."

"Then I should make sure to go with you to a party at some point," she responds.

My heart constricts at her words, hoping they mean that she thinks about spending time with me as much as I spend thinking about her. Maybe this is the right time to ask her on a date?

"Are you going out tonight? I could show you then." I ask the question despite knowing it's likely. Everyone goes out on Halloween, there's even a big pub crawl going on organised by one of the societies, though I can't remember which one. I think it's FaeSoc.

She shakes her head. "My plans for the night involve a good book and a hot cup of tea." Something in the way she says it makes me think there's more to it, but I don't know how to ask for the information without sounding like I'm prying.

"Ah, maybe next time?"

"Definitely."

The lecturer walks in before I get a chance to say anything else, ruining my chances of asking her on a date for another week. Why can't I just come out and say that I want to go on one? I know admitting I'm interested is likely to change things between us, but I doubt it'll do that much, especially if I make sure to not be unreasonable about it if she turns me down.

Juniper slides a piece of paper across to me and I notice that she's already started a game of boxes.

I smother a laugh and put my own line on the page, moving it back to her. It's a game I played a lot as a child when we went out for dinner, but rediscovered when I met Juniper. It's become something of a tradition between us now that our lectures have become too boring for us to pay much attention to.

We take a few more turns, sometimes taking a moment to pay attention to what's going on in front of us so we don't completely lose focus on what the lecture is about. Whether it's interesting or not, it's going to be part of our final exam and we'll need to study a lot of the theories that are talked about. Though perhaps our lack of concentration now will be useful for suggesting that Juniper joins me in a study session.

"Emmett?" she whispers.

"Hmmm?"

"It's your go, but you've been staring into space." She keeps her voice low, making it very unlikely that anyone can overhear.

"Sorry, I was thinking."

"About?"

"The fact we're going to have to study extra hard if we're going to try and pass our exam."

She lets out a soft snort. "We can find a way to make it fun."

"Do you have any ideas?"

"We can reward ourselves with ice cream. I'd suggest shots, but we want to be sober enough that the information will go in," she says.

"Excellent point. Ice cream it is. Will that be enough, though?"

"It's going to have to be unless we can find a *Marketing to Supernaturals for Dummies* book."

"If one doesn't exist, we should write it."

"I'm not sure I'd even know where to start," she admits. "Which is why I took this class in the first place." A hint of bitterness enters her voice.

"Same."

She lets out a loud sigh. "I suppose it'll still look good on our transcripts. But sometimes I get the feeling like that's all some classes are. Is this one really preparing me for the real world?"

"I suppose the question is would any of the others?"

"There's the cooking school," she points out. "And some of the other more specialised courses probably help."

"Do you wish you'd done one of them?"

"Not really. It would have limited my career options later. That's the hard part."

I nod along, completely understanding what she meant. I mostly came to the academy because I thought it was the next logical step for me, but while I enjoy life here, I'm not sure if it's actually the best for the future career that I want.

I suppose only time will tell if that's the case. I push the thought aside and turn my attention back to the game of boxes, adding a line that gives me five boxes in a row. Triumphantly, I scrawl an *E* in each box, marking them as points for me.

Juniper grins. "You fell right for my trap," she says, pulling the paper back and adding eleven boxes of her own, filling them with a much more elegantly written *J*. "I'd have thought you would have gotten wise to my tricks over the past couple of months."

"Maybe I'm letting you win."

"Nope, I can tell that's not it," she teases. "I'm winning fair and square."

The way she says it makes me certain she knows me well enough to be sure that what she's saying is true, and I like it. A lot. It makes me think that there could be something between us.

Now I just have to find the right time to do something about it.

THREE

Juniper

I HUM to myself as I head back into my flat. My lectures didn't get much better after the first one, but at least I got to see Emmett. I always come away from our interactions feeling good, but I can't put my finger on why. With him, something just clicks.

There's a part of me that wonders if there could be something more between us, but I don't ask for fear that I'll ruin the friendship we've managed to build for ourselves. He certainly makes my *Marketing to Supernaturals* lecture better than it would otherwise be. I might have tried to transfer out of it if it hadn't meant giving up the time we spent together too.

I push open the front door just as my stomach lets out a loud rumble. I'm not surprised by my need to eat, it's been a while since lunch and I haven't had time to pick up a snack. I head to the kitchen to grab one of my pumpkin cakes, certain there'll still be some left.

Sure enough, the covered plate I left out on the kitchen table is only half empty. I pull one of them out and bite into it, enjoying the spiced cake within. I close my eyes and savour the flavour. They're one of my better batches, which is good when I'm feeding them to my flatmates. Unlike carrot cake, a lot of how good these turn out is down to the pumpkin itself.

It'll only take the edge off my hunger, but it'll be enough for me to settle down and get comfortable before I have to face the task of making dinner. Though I shouldn't wait too long on that front, I'm sure my flatmates will want to use the kitchen for their pre-drinks, and I'd rather be safely locked in my room with my Jack-o'-lantern.

I step out of the kitchen and almost run straight into Thalia.

"Oh, Juniper, I'm really sorry," she says, pulling me out of my thoughts.

I frown. "For what?"

"Building services came." She gestures to my bedroom.

My heart sinks. "What did they do?"

"They took your pumpkin," she says softly. "I tried to convince them not to, but they were adamant."

"Why?" My voice cracks.

"I'm not sure, they said they'd put a notice in your room."

I bite my lip and nod, trying not to get too upset by the turn of events, especially when it isn't Thalia's fault.

"I know you need one for tonight, do you want me to stay and help carve it? I'm not sure how good I'll be..."

I shake my head. "It's fine," I assure her. "I'm fine. I'll just go get a new one. I'll have enough time if I get it now."

"Are you sure?"

"Enjoy your night," I say, trying to make sure she can tell from my tone that I mean it and don't expect her to change her plans just because of this.

"All right, but if you change your mind, message me?"

"I will." Though I know I won't need to.

She doesn't seem convinced, but nods anyway. "I

should make myself some dinner before pre-drinks start and I regret not eating."

I chuckle. "You really should."

"Your pumpkin cakes are delicious, by the way. I can't say I'm sad that we're going to end up with more of them."

I let out a soft snort. "Maybe I should send one down to building services to say thanks."

"I can't decide whether I think that's genius, or if I'm sad that we'll lose a cake in the process."

"Hmm, good point. There are still some of the original batch left if you want them, though."

"I should get going before the guys start drinking, they'll be gone as soon as they hit their fourth beer."

"We should hide them before that."

"I'll make it my sacred duty to ensure that they don't waste them."

"I don't mind if they do," I promise. "Especially if there'll be more pumpkin."

"Yes, but the rest of us care," she counters. "We want more of your cakes. I'm definitely going to go and get one now."

"Enjoy." I wave goodbye to her and head to my room, dreading the reasoning that building services is going to have given for getting rid of my pumpkin.

I push open my bedroom door and head straight

to my desk where the notice is sitting. I pick it up and scan the page.

Removed as a fire hazard.

"Eurgh." I scrunch the notice and throw it into the bin. "It wasn't even lit up." And it's not like the academy has a rule against lighting candles, I checked several times so I could be sure that I'd be able to do my Jack-o'-lantern without breaking any of the rules.

It seems like the rules aren't worth much anyway.

I try not to let it bother me. I still have a few hours before I really need it. I'll just head to the supermarket and pick up a new one. I haven't seen many around campus, which suggests there'll still be some, though I realise I'm cutting it fine at this time on Halloween itself.

But it isn't like I have another option. It's either try and get a new pumpkin now, or end up hiding for the whole time with the covers over my head, loud music blasting, and absolutely no sleep. That doesn't sound fun in the slightest to me.

I grab my purse from the bag I've been using all day and slip it into my coat pocket along with my phone. I need a new reusable bag anyway, so I'll get one at the supermarket.

I let out a deep sigh and head for the door. Maybe I'll treat myself to a coffee from Pixie Cups too. If

I'm heading in that direction anyway, then I may as well, and it might cheer me up after my building services mishap.

Either that, or it'll keep me up all night, but there's a chance of that happening anyway.

FOUR

Juniper

A group of students leave Magimarket with bags full of what I can only assume is stuff for pre-drinks, though from the hungry expression on the face of the vampire at the back, he might be after a can of blood. From what one of my brother's exes said, the Magimarket blood will do in a pinch and isn't very expensive, but the stuff that can be bought from proper vampire bars and shops is better.

I always assumed it was true, the pre-mixed potions they sell here are nowhere near as good as making it yourself, but when a hangover hits, sometimes the choice is an over-the-counter cure, or a coffee with a magical shot.

A soft whisper of indistinguishable voices fills the air around me, making the hair on the back of my neck stand on end. I hurry into the supermarket, realising that I'm cutting this finer than I'd like if I want to be able to spend a peaceful night without being constantly disturbed by the dead.

The bright lights are a harsh contrast to the almost darkness outside, but they quiet the whispers enough for me to focus on the task at hand.

I ignore the shelves of magical hair dye and deals on the latest flavour of alcopop and head to where the fruit and veg are normally found. Just a few days ago, there was a basket full to the brim of pumpkins, and while I suspect many of them have been bought already, I'm hoping that I'll be able to find at least one last one sitting at the bottom.

I turn the corner and my heart sinks as I come into view of the basket.

The very *empty* basket.

I take a deep breath, trying not to let the panic overtake me. There may not be any pumpkins here, but that doesn't mean there aren't some in the back. I hurry towards the tills, waiting impatiently behind a trio of giggling first-year students.

"Welcome to Magimarket," the bored cashier says.

"Hi, I was wondering if there were any more pumpkins?"

"The pumpkins are in the corner of the vegetable aisle." She gestures in the direction I've just come from.

"I know where they should be," I respond. "But there aren't any. Do you have more in the back?"

"It's Halloween," she says.

"Yes, it is. Do you have any pumpkins in the back?"

"No."

"Can you check?" I try to keep the panic building inside me out of my voice, but I don't do a very good job of it.

"It's Halloween," she repeats.

"I know it's Halloween." Frustration joins the despair.

"There aren't going to be any pumpkins left unless you want one that's deformed."

"I don't care what it looks like," I promise. "I just need a pumpkin."

She shrugs. "Fine, stay here." She disappears in the direction of the door to the back and I relax slightly.

I ignore the other people in the supermarket, mostly because I don't know any of the others I've passed, but also because I'm not in the mood to make small talk with anyone. Hopefully, my flatmates will be too busy getting ready for their night out by the time I get back and won't want to talk to me about all of this.

The woman returns quickly, making me wonder whether she's even looked, or if she just went into the back and waited long enough for me to think that she has.

"Is there one?" I ask. From her empty hands, I have to assume the answer is no, but I have to ask just in case I've got it wrong.

"No pumpkins."

"Do you know if the Magimarket across town will have one?" If I get a taxi, I should be able to get there and back within half an hour. Maybe.

The cashier gives me an incredulous look. "On Halloween?"

I let out a loud sigh. "I know it's Halloween," I retort. "That's why I need a pumpkin."

"I doubt they have one, but you're welcome to go look."

I give her a tight smile. "Thanks for your help." The words taste bitter as they leave my mouth, but I've been raised to be polite, even if I'm annoyed. And there's a chance she's done everything possible to try and help me, but just wasn't successful.

I make my way out of the supermarket and let

out a loud sigh, leaning against the wall and giving myself a moment to think. She didn't say that the other Magimarket *wouldn't* have a pumpkin, but her implication was that I'd be foolish to go all the way there.

Whispers start in the air around me, growing louder with each passing second. I screw my eyes shut, trying to stop it from getting to me.

"Go away," I murmur. "Away!"

"Juniper?"

I open my eyes, panic flaring through me as I find myself facing a confused-looking Emmett.

Great. Just the person I want to see when I'm close to losing my mind from the whispers.

"Are you okay?" he asks.

I take a deep breath and consider lying for a very brief moment, but decide I don't want to. There's something about Emmett that makes me want to be completely honest with him.

"No."

"Anything I can help with?" He leans against the wall with me, not close enough to touch, but almost.

A small part of me wishes for him to reach out.

Or a large part of me, if I'm being honest with myself.

"Do you have a pumpkin in your flat?" I ask.

He frowns. "As in the big orange vegetable people carve faces into?"

"They're actually fruit," I say needlessly. "But yes, one of those."

"I don't think so, unless a ceramic one counts, I think one of my flatmates put one in the kitchen."

I let out a small groan. "No, that doesn't count."

"Why not?"

"I've no idea, actually." I tried it a few years ago and it was the worst Halloween I'd had in my entire life.

"I take it you need to be able to carve it into a Jack-o'-lantern?"

I nod. "How do you know?"

"Lucky guess for what you might want one for on Halloween." He smiles at me, making me feel as if things aren't quite as hopeless as they could be, though I don't see how that's possible when I still don't have a pumpkin.

"Fair enough. But yes, I need a Jack-o'-lantern. I had one, but building services removed it as a fire hazard. It wasn't even lit."

"I'm sorry, that sucks."

"It does. We're allowed to burn candles. More to the point, I can just do this." I pull out my wand and give it a flick, creating an effortless flame between us.

Emmett chuckles and pulls out his own, sending a splash of water in the direction of the flame and extinguishing it effortlessly. "And that."

"*Exactly*. When there are students at the academy who can literally set fire to things with their mouths, why is one little candle a problem?"

"That's an interesting way of referring to dragon shifters."

"Only the fire-breathing ones, I know there are others who do other things."

"Hmm, true. I can never decide whether it would be better if one of them set fire to campus, or if one of them flooded it."

To my surprise, a small laugh escapes me. "Can you swim?"

"Yes. Why does that matter?"

"Because you're more likely to survive the flood than the fire if you can't get to your wand that way."

"Ah, good point," he concedes. "I take it your attempts at getting a pumpkin from Magimarket failed?"

I sigh. "Yep. She said there weren't any in the back, and that it was *highly unlikely* the other one across town would have one either."

"There are other supermarkets. We could try one of those?"

"Do you really think we'll find one?"

He grimaces, revealing what he thinks of the chances.

I let out a loud sigh. "I thought as much."

"But I do have an idea."

I frown. "What is it?"

"Do you trust me?"

"Yes." I don't even have to think about it. Of all the people I've met at Obscure Academy, he's the one I trust the most. And it isn't just because of how understanding and patient he's being right now, even if I haven't actually explained anything yet.

"Then wait here. I'll be back."

"Okay." Despite the soft whispers swirling in the air around me, his presence makes me feel as if I'm capable of dealing with the night to come.

Though whether that's going to be possible without a pumpkin remains to be seen.

FIVE

Emmett

THE EXPRESSION on Juniper's face makes my heart ache. I'm not sure why she's so desperate for a pumpkin, but I do know that there's a feeling inside me that's urging me to do everything I possibly can to make her feel better about the situation.

Magimarket is surprisingly empty for the time. I'm used to there being more students in here buying last-minute mixers or cheap wine. I actually came for the same thing myself. But now I have a different goal.

I head towards the fruit and vegetable section, already knowing that it was unlikely there would be a pumpkin there. From the despair in Juniper's voice, she'd already have it in her possession if there was one.

I scan the shelves, hoping the store is big enough to have what I want. Relief floods through me as I spot the telltale purple hue of a turnip. I pick the two biggest ones I can find out of the crate, turning them over in my hands so I can be certain they'll work for carving. I'm not sure if they'll be right for what Juniper needs them for, but I hope so.

It only takes me a few minutes to pay at the till and head back outside.

Juniper has her hands over her ears and appears to be singing to herself.

I clear my throat from a few feet away, not wanting to take her off guard and scare her. Somehow, I don't think that will help with my plan of eventually asking her out on a date.

She looks up and a small smile breaks over her face. "Did they have one after all?" she asks, nodding to my bag.

"Not quite." I hold it out for her and she looks inside, frowning slightly.

"A turnip?" she asks, the confusion on her face mirrored in her voice.

"Well, two turnips. I remembered a story my cousin used to tell me about the first Jack-o'-lantern and how it was made out of a turnip. I think it's an Irish story."

"Of course." She nods, seeming to understand. "Pumpkins aren't native here."

"I don't know if they'll work for what you need, but I thought it might be better than nothing?"

"Thank you." The way she smiles at me makes me feel as if I'm the only person in the world she can see. "I don't know if a turnip will work, but it's better to try, right?"

I nod.

"But why did you get two?"

"Ah." I rub the back of my neck, trying to think of the right way to say this without seeming creepy or over-eager. "I was thinking you might want company while you carve. It's okay if you don't."

Her whole face lights up. "You want to carve turnips with me?"

"If you want company, then I'd like that, yes."

To my surprise, she holds out her hand to me.

I reach out and take it, letting our fingers entwine and enjoying the way it feels.

A lot.

I've thought about this many times, but I never imagined it would happen as easily as this.

"Are you okay with coming back to mine to

carve?" she asks. "My flatmates are all heading for a night out, but they shouldn't bother us."

I nod. "That sounds good to me."

We start walking in the direction of the accommodation blocks.

"Weren't you supposed to be going out tonight as well?" she asks. "I'm not keeping you from something fun, right?"

"Hanging out with you is going to be fun," I point out.

"That's not what I asked."

I let out a low chuckle, amused by how easily she picked up on my evasion. "It's fine. I wasn't even going to go out tonight until one of my friends asked earlier, I'll just message him and tell him that I've had a better offer."

"Is carving turnips *really* a better offer than a night out?"

"Well, I've never carved a turnip before," I admit. "Maybe I'll find my true calling in life."

She lets out an amused snort. "I haven't carved one either. Maybe we should look up a tutorial of some kind?"

"Do you think it'll be that different from carving a pumpkin?"

"I'm honestly not sure."

"We'll figure it out," I say with certainty. "And this

is why I'm sure that this will be more fun than going on a night out."

"Because we don't know what we're doing with these?" She lifts the bag of turnips.

"Because the company is good."

"Oh." She glances away, but not before the nearest street lamp illuminates the soft blush spreading over her cheeks.

"So out of interest, can I carve anything I want into my turnip, or does it need to be something specific?" I ask to change the subject slightly.

"It's your turnip."

"And I'm a warlock, I know as well as you do that when it comes to magic, it's best to do things the way they're meant to be."

"That's fair," she agrees. "But the answer is, I don't know. I've always done a traditional face on my pumpkins. I suppose it's going to be even more traditional this year." She doesn't sound too sad about that, nor does she have the same horrified look as she did outside the supermarket, which I take to be a good thing.

"Then I'm going to have to do a lot of fast thinking," I respond.

She flashes me a happy-looking smile. "This is me, by the way." She gestures to the gate and lets go of my hand to dig in her pocket for her ID card. She swipes it against the gate and waits for the click. "I've never asked which of the blocks you live in."

"I'm in C." I gesture back across campus. "Which is a lot more annoying when I want to go to any of the shops."

"But better if you want The Red Phoenix."

"Hmm, true. That's good on pub quiz night."

"Is it? I've never been."

"Maybe we should go sometime?" I suggest.

"As a team of two?"

I shrug. "Why not? We're smart people."

"Unless someone asks us about *Marketing to Supernaturals*."

I let out a loud laugh. "Yes, except for then. But it isn't our fault we're not learning anything in the lectures."

"Mmhmm." She opens her flat door just as a loud cheer sounds from the kitchen.

"They've started early."

"Or right one time if they want to hit the end of the bar crawl."

"Ah, that makes sense."

"Do you want a drink? Tea? Coffee? Something harder?" she asks. "I was going to stop by Pixie Cups and then I forgot."

"I can go back."

She shakes her head. "It's good. I'll just get some tomorrow. So, drink?"

"Whatever you're having."

"Herbal tea it is," she says brightly.

I grimace, regretting my choice already.

She chuckles. "I'm only kidding, I was planning on having a spiced hot chocolate before I ran into you."

I relax slightly, glad I don't have to drink something I don't like just so I don't appear to be rude. "That sounds good."

"Great. I'm in room two, make yourself comfy." She gestures towards the door in question.

I smile at her, but she's already heading into the kitchen. With nothing else for it, I push open the door to her room and step inside. This isn't exactly how I hoped to be invited into Juniper's room, but in a lot of ways, it's better. I'm not sure exactly why she needs to carve a Jack-o'-lantern, but the way she's acting makes it seem as if it's important to her, and I'm glad that she's willing to share that with me.

But that means I need to be careful not to push her too far, and to let her tell me the reasoning behind what's going on in her own time. Even if my curiosity is reaching new levels while I wait.

SIX

JUNIPER

How is Emmett in my room?

Of all the times I've thought about this, I don't think I ever considered that he'd end up here because I couldn't find a pumpkin.

I shake my head to rid myself of my thoughts and pick up my mug of hot chocolate, disappointed to discover I've already finished it.

"There's nothing worse than realising there's none of your drink left," Emmett says, gesturing to it."

I let out a small laugh. "No, there isn't." I glance out of the window, though the sky looks no different than it did before. I'm not surprised by that, it's not like I can see the veil between the living and the dead, and there aren't many ghosts hanging around campus, thankfully. Probably something to do with there being enough reapers around to help them with their unfinished business.

"I can't believe you're making me do all of this by hand," Emmett says as he scoops out another clump of turnip. "I can safely say this is the first time I've ever done this."

"We can have turnip soup afterwards," I suggest.

He wrinkles his nose. "I'll pass. I don't like turnips very much."

"Me neither, it's another reason why a pumpkin would have been better."

"I'm sure there must be something nice we can make with it," he says.

"Honestly, that isn't my biggest concern right now."

"Ah, the need for a Jack-o'-lantern." He picks up one of the markers and starts drawing a face on his hollowed-out turnip. "Do you want to talk about it?"

I frown. Do I?

Even as I ask myself the question, I realise what the answer is.

"I can hear the dead on Halloween," I say. "Kind of."

He raises an eyebrow, but doesn't tell me it's impossible for me to do that. "Go on."

"It's nothing distinguishable, it's just loud whispering."

"Ah, so the voices are who you were telling to go away when I found you outside Magimarket."

I nod, appreciating his observational skills. "Sometimes, it gets too much."

"And the Jack-o'-lanterns help?"

"It's what my family has always done. They're supposed to keep the evil spirit's away, and it works. At least, I think it does. I never feel the voices around me as strongly when I have one burning." I glance out of the window again.

Emmett follows my gaze, trying to spot something that isn't there. "What causes it?"

"I'm not sure. It's a problem my entire family has. My brother thinks we have reaper blood or something, but I know that isn't possible with how supernatural genetics work."

He frowns. "No, but necromancer might be."

I blink a few times. "Necromancer?"

"I'm sure you've heard the theory about all the different kinds of magic users originally being different species, right?"

"The one where a mage, a witch, and a warlock would all be different things?"

"That's the one," he says, excitement filling his voice. "It's a theory people are becoming more convinced about, especially after the discovery in Morocco about a year ago."

"What discovery?"

"I'll send you a link later," he promises. "But basically, some genetic experts have done studies that suggested the only reason necromancers didn't end up combined with the rest was because they'd already started hiding from the vampires."

"Which means that they didn't procreate with everyone else as much," I supply, scooping out the last of my turnip.

Emmett holds the pen out to me and I reach out to take it, our fingers brushing against one another as I do. My breathing hitches and soft tingles run across my skin.

He clears his throat, clearly as affected by the situation as I am. There's something reassuring about that.

"Anyway, what I was thinking was that maybe some necromancer blood did get mixed in with your family's at some point, and that's why this happens."

"In which case it's annoyingly watered down," I joke. "But I think the theory makes sense. From what Grandma used to tell me, the problem became weaker through the generations. I suppose there's not really a way to test it, though."

"Probably not, I imagine the genetics are too watered down to be able to see if you have a necromancer gene." He searches through my carving equipment to find the right knife to make the face.

"Otherwise, they'd have been able to prove the magic wielder theory," I say, picking up the one that I think will suit him best. I hand it to him, noticing that he seems to brush our fingers against one another on purpose this time.

I glance away and bite my bottom lip, unable to help the barrage of thoughts about how much I like it when he touches me.

In an attempt to distract myself, I focus on my turnip, carving a toothy smile and triangle eyes into the surface. It's not dissimilar to carving a pumpkin, but somehow, the result is both scarier and cuter at the same time.

"I think I'm done," Emmett says after ten more minutes. "Do you have any tealights?"

"Bottom drawer, unless building services got them too."

He lets out an amused snort and opens it, pulling out two tealights and setting one down next to me before placing the other inside his turnip. He points his wand towards the wick and lets a small flame burst forth. He sets it on my desk, letting the flickering light fill the room.

"I'm done too," I say, following suit and putting my tealight inside.

I set my turnip on my desk next to his and take a few steps back, running into Emmett in the process.

He puts an arm out to steady me, but doesn't pull it back once he's sure I'm stable.

"What do you think?" he asks.

"About?"

"Whether the Jack-o'-lanterns are working," he prompts.

"Oh, right." I've been too busy thinking about him to properly consider what we're supposed to be thinking about. I frown and do something I'm not sure I ever have before.

I try to hear the voices of the dead.

"And?" Emmett prompts after a few moments pass.

"I think it's silent," I whisper, touching the side of my head as if that's going to change anything. "It's actually silent."

"Is that normal?"

I shake my head. "The Jack-o'-lanterns help, but they aren't perfect," I admit. "But these ones have worked really well."

"Maybe turnips have been the answer all along," he jokes.

"I need to tell my family." I pull out my phone and snap a photo, typing out an explanation while Emmett smiles at me, seeming pleased that his suggestion has worked so well. I let out a loud sigh and turn to face him. "Thank you."

I give in to the urge to go up on my toes and press a kiss against his cheek.

"You're welcome." He touches his fingers to the spot I kissed. "I guess I should leave you to it, unless..."

"Unless?" I ask, hope filling me at the possibility of what he might be about to suggest.

"I was just thinking that if you didn't have any other plans, maybe we could hang out some more?"

My heart skips a beat. "I'd like that." The words are out of my mouth before I've even thought about it. When it comes to Emmett, I don't think there's any question in my mind about whether I want to spend more time with him.

"Great, are you hungry? I'm starved."

"Me too, I haven't eaten properly yet. I was going to, but then..." I wave my hand towards the turnips.

He nods in understanding. "We can order something?"

"I'd like that."

"How about I go pick up some pizza? That way we get it quicker."

My stomach grumbles, as if agreeing with his plan. "Sounds good."

"I'll be back."

"Wait, take my keycard." I hand it to him. "I know we're not supposed to, but it'll stop me from having to leave the protection of the room."

"Good idea." He takes it from me, then hesitates as if he wants to say something else. He must decide better of it, as he flashes me one last smile and leaves the room.

I sigh and flop onto my bed, enjoying the peace that the turnips are giving me.

Or maybe it isn't them, but the fact that I have something new to focus on instead of the voices of the dead outside my window.

SEVEN

Juniper

A cool breeze comes in through the window, causing me to shiver and the flames within the turnips to flutter. Despite that, they both stay burning strong. One of the many advantages of magical flames.

Emmett reaches out and puts an arm around me. I take advantage of it to move closer and rest my head against his shoulder.

"I have to admit, I never thought you'd want to put Halloween movies on," he admits.

I let out a small laugh. "I never said I didn't like Halloween."

"Hmm. True. So everything that can be done in

the safety of your room is fine, even if it's Halloweeny?"

"Yes. Why?" I ask, wondering what he's getting at.

"Erm..."

"Emmett?"

"I was trying to think of a fun way to ask you on a date that was related to *trick or treat*, but I failed so badly that now I'm admitting it to you."

Amusement darts through me. "So instead, you're asking me on a date by saying that you wanted to ask me on a date but haven't found the right way to?"

"Precisely."

"I'd like that. A date."

His whole face lights up. "You would?"

"Definitely. But I do have a question?" I sit up, regretting that it brings me away from his embrace, but appreciating that it lets me properly see him.

"Hmm?"

"Wouldn't this count as a date? We've had dinner, watched a movie, hung out alone..."

"We haven't kissed though," Emmett replies.

"So if we did kiss, then this would also count as a date?" I'm sure my amusement is coming through my tone, but I think that's okay given the situation.

His eyes widen. "I've barely managed to ask you on a date, I'm not sure I'm going to be able to ask if I can kiss you all in the same night."

"So what if I asked? You did the date, I can do the kiss." I cock my head to the side. "Unless you don't want to."

"I want to." His gaze drops to my lips, which is all the confirmation I need that he's telling the truth.

"Then I'd really like it if we kissed and turned this into a proper date." My heart pounds, but in a good way, like my whole body can already tell that what's ahead is going to be something special.

Emmett shifts on the bed so we're facing one another, but pulls a face.

"What is it?"

"I had garlic bread," he admits.

"I did too," I remind him. "But I'm not a vampire, you can kiss me even if you've had garlic."

"I don't think they're actually allergic to it."

"I imagine if a turned vampire was allergic to garlic before they became a vampire then they'd still be. Does vampirism remove allergies?"

"I have no idea," Emmett admits. "But are you rambling to stall?"

"I'm nervous, but in a good way."

"Me too." He reaches out and touches my cheek, causing a flutter of anticipation to build within me. I lean in, my eyes falling shut as I feel the warmth of his breath against my lips.

All of my nerves flee as I realise that this is exactly how things are meant to be.

The moment his lips brush against mine, I realise just how right I am. I reach out and wrap my arms around his neck, pulling him closer and deepening our kiss in the process. He puts a hand on the small of my back, and the other threads into my hair.

It's impossible to keep track of anything other than Emmett during our kiss. It's like time stands still and the world disappears and all of those other clichés that go along with a first kiss that just feels right.

He breaks our kiss, a wide grin on his face.

"Is it a date now?" I ask, my voice a little hoarse.

"Definitely a date now," he responds. "I hope there's a second."

"Kiss or date?"

"Both."

"Good." I settle back into his arms while the film continues to play in the background. "Thank you for keeping me company tonight."

"You're welcome."

"No one's ever done that before," I admit.

"Kept you company?"

"Not on Halloween. Well, I suppose my family has, but no one but them has ever really known about my problem to know to stay with me. Thalia, my flatmate, stayed with me last year, though I think that was as much for her as it was for me."

"Is it supposed to be a secret?"

I shake my head. "I don't think so, but it's not something anyone in my family has ever talked about."

"Well, I'm glad you told me," he says. "And that I could help."

"You helped a lot, the turnips were a genius idea. I think they're working even better than the pumpkin would have."

"Is it because there's two of them, or because they're turnips?"

"I'm not sure," I admit. "It could also be that I'm more distracted than normal."

"In which case, I'm happy to supply turnips and distractions for this year, and future ones."

I raise an eyebrow. "You only just managed to ask me on a date and now you're talking about future Halloweens?"

"Mmhmm. There's no point going on a date with someone you don't see a future with. And there's a reason I've been worrying about asking you on a date, I was worried about how it might ruin things and I wasn't ready for that. I like you a lot, Juniper. I've liked you since the moment we met."

I reach up and tuck a strand of dark hair behind

my ear. "It's the same for me. I'd always like it when I found myself sitting next to you."

"That's because our lecture is really dull and I'm the most entertaining choice in the room," he teases.

"You are to me." I lean my head against his shoulder and sigh. "Well, I'm grateful for our dreadfully dull lecture."

"We're going to end up looking back fondly on M2S, aren't we?"

I let out a small snort. "If you continue to kiss like that, it might end up being my favourite lecture."

"Then I will do my best." The happiness on his face makes it clear that he means the words.

And I'm sure I'm smiling back just as broadly. This is easily my best Halloween night to date.

EIGHT

Emmett

I ignore the hustle and bustle of Pixie Cups behind me as I search the approaching faces for Juniper. I'm eager to hear how she got on with the turnips after I left last night, and hopeful that they worked just the way they should.

I finally spot her and lift my hand to wave, smiling broadly. Even from this distance, I can see her face light up as she spots me in return.

"Morning," I say.

"Morning." She goes onto her toes and presses her lips against mine.

I'm surprised for the briefest moment, thinking that she might not want to go straight into this part of a relationship. Not that I'm complaining. I like the idea that she's so comfortable with me.

Juniper pulls back and flashes me a shy smile.

"I take it the turnips worked, then," I say.

She gives a soft laugh. "They did, but the kiss was because I wanted to, not because I'm grateful for your turnips."

"You shouldn't say that too loudly, people might think it means something completely different," I joke.

A blush rushes to her cheeks, making me wonder whether I've overstepped the line.

"What would they...oh. Oh. I can't believe I didn't think of that."

I let out an amused laugh. "I'm half surprised you didn't do it on purpose."

"I'll have to get better at that if you're going to keep using vegetable jokes."

"Or fruit jokes," I retort.

"Except that turnips *are* vegetables."

"Well that's just confusing. We're carving pumpkins that are fruits, or turnips that are vegetables. Why can't people choose?" I push the door to Pixie Cups open and hold it open so she can pass.

She reaches out and brushes my arm as she passes, presumably as a gesture of thanks.

"I imagine most people just carved their Jack-o'-lantern into the nearest fruit or vegetable with the right kind of skin," she says. "It's not all that different from what we did last night."

"Ah, no wonder it worked, then. Maybe that was it and not the material." We join the small queue of students who are all in desperate need of a caffeine fix. Some more than others if the guy nursing a hangover right in front of us is anything to go by.

"Honestly, I don't mind *why* it worked, I'm just happy it did," Juniper says. "I actually got some decent sleep after you left."

"No voices?" I check, wanting to make sure I understand her properly.

She shakes her head. "Not a peep."

"I realised that I never actually asked, but what do they say?" I was too distracted by making sure she was getting what she needed and didn't think to question exactly how it works.

"I don't know. That's one of the things that's made the whole thing so unmanageable. If I could hear them properly, then I could help them." She lets out a loud sigh, proving the truth behind her words. Not that I'd ever doubt them, she's clearly the kind of person who would do anything she could if she felt someone was in need.

"Ah, but because you can't, there's nothing you can do," I respond.

She nods. "It's frustrating. It's not that I don't want to help, just that I can't. Grandma tried a lot of things, including exorcism."

"That's extreme." I don't think I know anyone who would go through with that voluntarily, especially not a witch. The covens all have a healthy distrust of anything that even hints at the way the witch hunts used to be run.

"She wanted to stop the voices. I've never been tempted enough myself, but I can't hear them as strongly as she could. She'd still have been able to hear them for the next few days, whereas everything is silent now for me," Juniper explains.

I nod in understanding. "Interesting."

The queue moves, allowing us to reach the front. I smile at the barista and turn to Juniper. "What do you want?"

"A pumpkin spice latte with a shot of alertness, please," she says.

"I'll have the same," I say. "Though I didn't expect you to abandon *Team Turnip* so easily."

A soft snort escapes from Juniper. "It's *Team Turnip* for Jack-o'-lanterns, *Team Pumpkin* for taste." She pulls her bank card out of her pocket at the same time I go for mine. "You paid for the turnips," I remind him.

I consider trying to argue with her, but I can tell from her face that she's determined to pay.And it's not like I'm going to have plenty of opportunity to pay for my share of drinks and dinners if we continue to date, and I certainly hope that will be the case.

"Have you found something to do with the turnip innards yet?" I ask once she's done.

"One of my flatmates has taken them for her cooking class. She says she's going to use it as a challenge for the students."

"She teaches?" My surprise comes through my voice.

"It's part of the cooking school curriculum, I think. As part of it, the cookery students have to teach a night school class."

"Interesting," I muse. "I didn't realise."

"Presumably because you've never been to the cooking school," Juniper points out.

"I'd like to think that I don't need the lessons." Though maybe I should do now I have someone to impress with my cooking.

"Not having tasted your cooking, I'd have no way of knowing."

"Is that you angling for an invitation to

57

homemade dinner?" I hope she says yes. I don't even know what I'd make, I just know that I want to spend the time with her.

"It wasn't, actually. I figured that if we continue dating, we'll end up cooking for each other fairly often. I doubt either of us can afford eating out all the time."

"Mmm, the plight of being a student," I agree. "All of the money goes on textbooks and fancy coffees."

A pair of takeaway cups float towards us, hanging in the air until we grab them. I take a moment to appreciate the magic, even if I don't know precisely how it's being done.

Juniper glances in the direction of the barista as if she's trying to work it out herself, which makes me even more certain that she's a good match for me.

"Do you want to sit or walk?" I ask when she turned back to me.

Juniper lets out a loud sigh. "We need to walk, we have a seminar to get to, remember?"

"I'd forgotten," I admit. "And I hate cutting our time together short."

"It is a short second date."

"This is our second date already?" Dare I hope that she wants to spend as much time with her as I do with her?

"What did you think it was?" she asks sweetly.

"Coffee."

"It can be just coffee if you want. Or it can be our second date, and tonight I could come around and see your place for our third."

"What happens on our third date?" She seems excited for the prospect of it, but I'm not sure precisely why. She must have some idea in mind.

"Whatever we want to. Dating rules are just for people who don't know if they like each other yet."

I let out a short laugh. "I haven't heard that one before."

"Probably because that's just my excuse for throwing all of the rules out of the window," she admits. "But the point is a valid one. We should go at a pace that suits us. It doesn't matter if that's fast or slow, it just has to be comfortable to me and to you."

"Ah, the turnips have made you wise," I quip.

"They have," she responds in a grave voice. "No one should ignore the wisdom of Turnip-Juniper."

I let out a low chuckle and reach out to take her free hand with mine. It's so easy to be around her that it feels natural to already be progressing to this stage with her. Then again, she already decided to kiss me hello, so maybe we're just going at her pace.

"I don't think anyone else is going to understand why you're Turnip-Juniper though," I point out.

"Hmm, true. But maybe I'll make a bigger thing of

it next year and get everyone to make turnip lanterns instead. I'll convert them all to *Team Turnip,* even if it means no pumpkin cakes."

"That is a shame, maybe I need to convert you back," I muse. Her pumpkin cakes were delicious. "Or maybe we can just make both."

"That sounds like a good solution." She leans in and kisses my cheek.

I grin broadly as we make our way through campus. If only I'd thought to ask her on a date sooner, then we might have shared more moments like this already. But that's not the end of the world. Not when I'll have plenty of future moments to spend with Juniper.

EPILOGUE

Juniper

The Following September

Emmett makes his way over to me through the crowd of witches and warlocks who have turned up for the first WitchSoc meeting of the year. I don't think I've seen this many members of the society in one room since this time last year. And in all likelihood, I won't again until next year. A lot of people come and go to meetings as their schedules allow, myself included.

"Hey," he says when he gets to me, putting his arm around my waist.

I step closer and lean against him. "Good day?" I ask.

He nods. "My electives this year sound much more interesting than M2S."

"And yet that's still going to end up being your favourite lecture in years to come."

"Without a doubt." There isn't a hint of amusement in his voice. He's serious about it.

Which makes sense, I am too.

"Juniper!" a familiar voice calls.

I turn to find Thalia's friend, Michaela, hurrying towards me with a dark-haired warlock in tow.

"I'm so glad you're here, Thalia said you would be when I called by your flat," she says.

"You were looking for me?" I can't keep the surprise out of my voice. I like Michaela, but we haven't spent all that much time around each other. She seems to be very friendly with her flatmates, and close with Thalia, and I have friends of my own.

"I've been asked to put on a charity event for WitchSoc next month and I have no idea what to do. They want it to be on Halloween of all days, but it's just not enough time to get a Haunted House next year, though maybe for next year." Her words almost tumble over one another as she gets them out, making it clear how stressed this is making her. "Anyway, I was wondering if you could help?"

"We'd love to," Emmett says. "Have you considered doing some Jack-o'-lantern carving?"

Michaela's eyes light up. "That's a great idea. And we can have a competition. We had one at my school once where everyone voted with money."

"How does that work?" I ask.

"You line up the Jack-o'-lanterns and put cups in front of them, then people throw in money for the one they think is the best, and the one with the highest amount in it wins."

"Ah, then the money goes to the charity." It makes sense when she puts it like that.

"Exactly. It's a great idea. I'm just going to go clear it with Cerise, but I don't see her saying no. Thanks." She smiles widely and waves goodbye to us, heading through the crowd to find the WitchSoc treasurer.

I turn to Emmett. "Jack-o'-lantern carving? How long have you been sitting on that one?"

"You said last year that we should convert everyone to turnips, what better way than a Jack-o'-lantern competition? I've been practising."

I shake my head in bemusement.

"Besides, I thought it would be a good way for you to be involved with a Halloween activity without having to worry about the veil. You'll be surrounded by dozens of Jack-o'-lanterns, so all you'll have to focus on is having a good time," Emmett says.

A wave of affection floods through me. I can't believe how much thought he's put into this. "I love you," I say as I wrap my arms around his neck.

"I love you too," he responds, already leaning in so he can brush his lips against mine.

I melt into him despite the other people in the room. Most of them aren't paying us any attention anyway.

We break apart, and I slip my hand into his, enjoying how natural and normal it feels for us to show affection like this now. It's both hard to believe we've been together for nearly a year, and it makes perfect sense at the same time. I don't think anyone could ever make me feel as safe and heard as Emmett does.

Michaela pushes back through the crowd with an excited expression on her face, which only becomes stronger when she spots us.

"Cerise says it sounds like a good plan. We're going to be organising a pumpkin carving event on Halloween," she says brightly.

"Not just pumpkins," Emmett says. "There should be turnips too."

"Turnips?" Michaela asks.

"They're traditional," I say by way of explanation.

"We carved them last year when I couldn't find any pumpkins."

"Then we can do turnips too. I bet they'll be cheaper to get than pumpkins too. But should we have a prize for the best turnip and best pumpkin, or just for the best Jack-o'-lantern?" she muses.

"How about three prizes," I suggest. "One for a turnip, one for a pumpkin, and one for any other fruit or vegetable that someone wants to use to carve one."

"A coconut Jack-o'-lantern would be fun," Emmett muses.

I let out a small groan. "What have I done?"

"Made his day, apparently," Michaela quips.

"Or I've lost him to an entire day walking around Magimarket trying to work out what he might be able to carve a face into," I retort.

"I like how you're pretending you're not going to be right there with me," he says.

"I'll be sticking to turnips this year," I promise him.

"Oh, then I'll do a pumpkin, then we'll each be doing one of the categories," Michaela says. "This couldn't have worked out more perfectly."

"It really couldn't," I say, looking at Emmett with a serene smile on my face. It felt like everything was going to go wrong the moment building services took my pumpkin, but in reality, that led to something even better.

* * *

THANK you for reading *Pumpkin Carving For Superstitious Witches,* I hope you enjoyed it! If you want to read more about the witches at Obscure Academy, then you can in Michaela's story, *Potion Making For Disastrous Witches*: http://books2read.com/potionmakingfordisastrouswitches

If you want to read Juniper's version of chapter 8, then you can download it for free here: https://books.authorlauragreenwood.co.uk/9xjh7svgo6

AUTHOR NOTE

Thank you for reading *Pumpkin Carving For Superstitious Witches*, I hope you enjoyed it!

Do you prefer the idea of carving a pumpkin or a turnip? You can vote for which team you support on my website: https://www.authorlauragreenwood.co.uk/p/pumpkin-carving.html (it's just a little bit of fun!)

If you want to know more about Thalia, then you can find her in *Blind Dates For Lonely Gorgons*, which follows Thalia and her boyfriend (Evander) as they get together after a blind dating event.

Or, if you want more witches from Obscure Academy, you can find Michaela and Owen in *Potion Making For Disastrous Witches*, which follows Michaela when she needs Owen's help in order to successfully brew a potion (something she's not very good at!)

And there will be more witches and warlocks in future Obscure Academy books too - as well as appearances from both Juniper and Emmet as side characters.

If you're wondering about the pumpkin cakes that Juniper makes, then they're real! I discovered the recipe one year when my Dad and youngest brother decided they wanted a lot of pumpkins and we ended up with a lot of spare pumpkin flesh and I was desperate *not* to eat more pumpkin soup. The cake was delicious, and I've made it again since - if you like carrot cake, I'd highly recommend giving it a try (you can download the recipe here!)

Or, if it's the Halloween theme you want more of, why not try *Accidental Cupid*, a standalone in the *Supernatural Retrieval Agency* series that follows Pippa as she tries to avoid matchmaking anyone at her friends' engagement & Halloween party.

If you want to keep up to date with new releases and other news, you can join my Facebook Reader Group or mailing list.

Stay safe & happy reading!

- Laura

ALSO BY LAURA GREENWOOD

Signed Paperback & Merchandise:

You can find signed paperbacks, hardcovers, and merchandise based on my series (including stickers, magnets, face masks, and more!) via my website: https://www.authorlauragreenwood.co.uk/p/shop.html

Series List:

* denotes a completed series

The Obscure World

A paranormal & urban fantasy world where supernaturals live out in the open alongside humans. Each series can be read on its own, but there are cameos from past characters and mentions of previous events.

Cauldron Coffee Shop - Broomstick Bakery - Obscure Academy - The Shifter Season - Ashryn Barker* - Grimalkin Academy* - City Of Blood* - Grimalkin Vampires* - Supernatural Retrieval Agency* - The Black Fan* - Sabre Woods Academy* - Scythe Grove Academy*

* * *

The Forgotten Gods World

A fantasy romance world based on Egyptian mythology. Each series can be read on its own, but there are cameos from past characters and mentions of previous events.

Forgotten Gods - The Queen of Gods* - Forgotten Gods: Origins*

* * *

The Egyptian Empire

A modern fantasy world set in an alternative timeline where the Egyptian Empire never fell.

The Apprentice Of Anubis

* * *

The Paranormal Council World

A paranormal romance & urban fantasy world where paranormals are hidden away from the human world, and are in search of their fated mates. Each series can be read on its own, but there are cameos from past characters and mentions of previous events.

The Paranormal Council Series* - The Fae Queens* - Paranormal Criminal Investigations* - The Necromancer Council* - Return Of The Fae*

* * *

Other Series

Purple Oasis (with Arizona Tape) - Grimm Academy - Beyond The Curse* - Untold Tales* - The Dragon Duels* - Speed Dating With The Denizens Of The Underworld (shared world) - Seven Wardens* (with Skye MacKinnon) - Tales Of Clan Robbins (co-written with L.A. Boruff) - Firehouse Witches* (with Lacey Carter Andersen & L.A. Boruff) - Valentine Pride* (with Lainie Anderson) - Magic and Metaphysics Academy* (with Lainie Anderson)

* * *

Twin Souls Universe

A paranormal romance & urban fantasy world co-written with Arizona Tape. Each series can be read on its own, but there are cameos from past characters and mentions of previous events.

Amethyst's Wand Shop Mysteries - Twin Souls* - The Vampire Detective*

ABOUT LAURA GREENWOOD

Laura is a USA Today Bestselling Author of paranormal, fantasy, urban fantasy, and contemporary romance. When she's not writing, she drinks a lot of tea, tries to resist French macarons, and works towards a diploma in Egyptology. She lives in the UK, where most of her books are set. Laura specialises in quick reads, whether you're looking for a swoonworthy romance for the bath, or an action-packed adventure for your latest journey, you'll find the perfect match amongst her books!

Follow the Author

- Website: www.authorlauragreenwood.co.uk
- Mailing List: www.authorlauragreenwood.co.uk/p/mailing-list-sign-up.html
- Facebook Group: http://facebook.com/groups/theparanormalcouncil

- Facebook Page: http://facebook.com/authorlauragreenwood
- Bookbub: www.bookbub.com/authors/laura-greenwood

Printed in Poland
by Amazon Fulfillment
Poland Sp. z o.o., Wrocław